Fun Physical Fitness for the Home

by Sono Sato Harris

© Copyright 1992 by Sono Sato Harris.

Published by Noble Publishing Associates
Vancouver WA 98685

Phone 1-800-225-5259

Printed in China

1 2 3 4 5 6 7 8 9

ISBN 1-56857-036-8

Note: The author and publisher are not liable for any injury or death incurred due to the misuse of the suggested materials and directions. As with all child-related activities, materials should be selected with careful attention to child safety; adult supervision is essential.

FOREWORD

Welcome to a fun program of physical fitness that you can start in your home today! I am excited about this updated version with the new Supplemental Exercises Section. Added to the original Fun Fitness Program with music tape, they comprise my all time favorite strengthening and stretching exercises for children, ages two and up.

These exercises help children develop coordination, strength, flexibility and stamina. I have created some and collected others over the years as a student, performer and teacher of ballet, modern dance, creative dance and gymnastics.

The good news is that you don't have to be a professional dancer or P.E. major to use them with your children. These exercises are simple, easily learned and executed in the home. My son Joshua's drawings make it is easy to follow the clear, step-by-step directions. The music tape done by Craig Bidondo, provides a wonderfully motivational dimension to over twenty exercises.

This program began to develop as I met our firstborn son Joshua's need for physical activity in our very little two bedroom home during the long winter months. Although I was teaching fourteen dance classes a week at the time, including an all boys class at the professional school for the Dayton Ballet Company, I knew it would be more effective if I worked with Josh at home. All aspects seemed consistent with our decision to home school: low ratio of students to teacher, no negative peer interaction, no chauffeuring and cost effective. So, besides one season on the soccer team, Josh's P.E. training was done at home.

At eleven he had a desire to take gymnastics, and we felt he was ready. He progressed rapidly and started competing his first year, capturing first place in the state of Oregon in his class. That same year he won a position on a team that travelled to Sapporo, Japan, where he placed first in five out of six events and received the All-Around title. The next year his coach had him skip a class (that's like going from 5th grade to 7th grade in academic terms!), and he managed to finish second in the state and fifth in the region.

Now, this experience does not mean that everyone who uses these exercises will necessarily produce great athletes. Natural gifting, desire and determination are also critical. But it does demonstrate that parents can do things at home that will make a positive difference. You can enhance each child's body awareness and coordination, maintain and increase his natural flexibility and strengthen his body's major muscle areas.

Five children and seventeen years later, I am still amazed at what a simple program like this can accomplish. Quite naturally, the four younger ones started observing, imitating and participating in their own modified version of the program at about age 18 months. When they are ready, I spend time instructing them in more of the details of each exercise.

Alex, Brett, Sarah and Isaac beg, "Can we do Fun Fitness?" Sometimes I will oversee the entire workout from start to finish, giving instruction and correction, encouraging and directing traffic. Often I can't join them, and they do it by themselves. That's another advantage of the program. After a certain degree of mastery is achieved, it can be a do-it-yourself aerobic workout. Many moms have written and told me that they do the exercises with their children for their own workout!

It is hard to believe that anything so fun could be so good for your body, but it really is! I hope you and your family enjoy using these exercises as much as we have.

Sono Sato Harris, April 1997

Table of Contents

Exercises with Musical Accompaniment

TABLE OF CONTENTS

Supplemental Exercises

Exercises with Musical Accompaniment

The Russian Bear

The Russian Bear is a crawl done on hands and feet, working up to straight knees and feet flat on the floor. It strengthens the arms, shoulders and thorax and stretches the back of the legs.

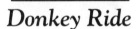

The Crab Crawl

The Crab Crawl is another crawl on hands and feet with the chest facing up towards the ceiling. The challenge is to push the weight up high so that the torso is flat as a table top (no drooping bottoms). It's a fun crawl to speed up as coordination allows and gives the feeling of scurrying like a sand crab on the beach. This crawl strengthens the upper body and hips and helps develop coordination.

Donkey Ride

In Donkey Ride the child begins seated with legs bent and open as if riding a donkey and arms forward as if holding reins. The poem is recited. Stretch forward as far as possible on first three lines and then roll back as if to do a back somersault but only roll to the shoulders and kickup legs with a big gallop for each 'hee-haw.' Donkey Ride is an overall body stretch.

I went for a ride in the country,
And what do you think I saw?
I saw a donkey eating and he said,
Hee-haw, hee-haw.

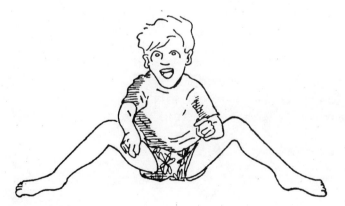

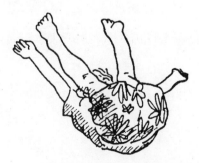

Blast Off!

Blast Off is a favorite with children because they get to be loud. The child starts in the frog sit position with his back "rocket ship" straight. The best way for mother to obtain a good, straight back is by standing behind the child and using the outside of the calf against his back and a hand on the chest to press him gently into a good upright position. The child then counts down from ten to zero as he slowly rounds his back over his legs (touching his nose to his toes) on "Blast off!" He puts one hand down near his seat and pushes himself up to an one hand-two feet balance. For an extra challenge have the child lift one leg off the floor and balance on the remaining hand and foot. This is hard. The trick is to stretch hard & lift the weight up. Blast off strengthens and stretches the body.

10-9-8-

7-6-5-

4-3-2-1-

0, BLAST OFF!

Swordfish

Swordfish is a fun but difficult exercise for the abdomen. It also provides a great mental picture for straight legs. We use "swordfish straight legs" as key words to remind them of the stretched leg position they use in Swordfish during other movement activities. The child begins seated, resting on his elbows. He lifts one 'swordfish' (a straight leg) and takes it swimming in the ocean. It is caught by a fisherman (the child grabs his own leg at the knee with both hands, thereby sitting up taller).

"A swordfish is out swimming happily in the ocean. He is carefree, diving down to the bottom of the ocean floor and shooting up to the surface. Again and again. He swims all over, here and there. Now he becomes curious about something he sees… Oh no!! He's been caught by a fisherman!"

All say together…
> *Let me go,*
> *Let me go,*
> *Let me go…. FREE!*

The swordfish says, "Let me go, let me go, let me go… FREE!!" The leg, released from the hands, taps the floor and rebounds back up once each on the words 'Let' and 'me' and lifts up and is held again on each ' go.' Then on 'free' the hands let go of the leg and the child holds it up unsupported for several seconds. Repeat with the other leg. The big challenge is next… the third time the exercise is done with both legs at the same time. Get ready to work! The two swordfish can be friends and swim together in the ocean blue. Sometimes they will fight. Do Criss-Cross Apple Sauce legs several times. (See page 23)

The Swordfish Script

After the children gain strength, it turns into a friendly contest to see who can hold that last position the longest on "FREE!!"

Parent narrates:

    A swordfish is out swimming happily in the ocean. He is carefree, diving down to the bottom of the ocean floor and shooting up to the surface. Again and again. He swims all over, here and there. Now he becomes curious about something he sees... Oh no!! He's been caught by a fisherman!

All say together...

    Let me go,
    Let me go,
    Let me go.... FREE!

Parent narrates:

    Another swordfish (same as above)

All say together...

    Let me go,
    Let me go,
    Let me go.... FREE!

Parent narrates:

    The two swordfish are now friends. What fun it is for them to explore the ocean together. They swim up to the surface and dive down to the bottom of the ocean together. Oh, dear, they are quarreling. Now they are fighting! Each goes its own way, one to the left and one to the right. Swimming alone again. They decide to make up, and they're swimming together again. They are going up near the surface and, whoops, they've been caught!

All say together...

    Let me go,
    Let me go,
    Let me go.... FREE!

But they make up eventually and dive down to the bottom of the sea and up again. Whoops! They get caught together!

This part is the same as with a single leg, but it's a lot harder to lift two legs. Be prepared for toppling over forwards, backwards and sideways.

All say together...

    Let me go,
    Let me go,
    Let me go.... FREE!

The Shoulder Sequence

The Shoulder Sequence is a five-part exercise
that is a challenging marathon for the upper
body:

1. Start in the push-up position. Actual push-ups can be executed
or hold the position (increasing number of push ups or extending amount
of time to hold as strength increases). A good place to start is half the
number of push ups the child is already able to do or a hold of thirty
seconds.

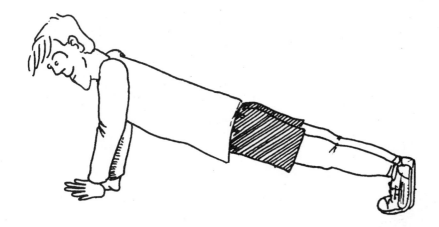

2. Go immediately into a one-hand, two-feet balance, torso facing
sideways, and keeping the supporting arm straight, allow the weight to
sag to the floor and then lift it up again; work up to ten.

Go immediately into the crab-crawl position and crawl. In a large room the child can crawl to the other end of the room. In a smaller room he can crawl forward to one end and then backward to the starting place.

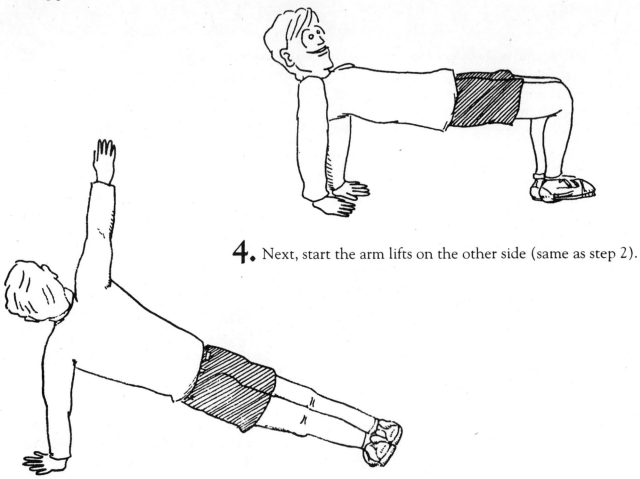

4. Next, start the arm lifts on the other side (same as step 2).

5. Return to the push-up position hold or push-ups. Do the same amount as in step 1. The difficulty of this sequence is in going straight from the one part to the next. No rest breaks in between!

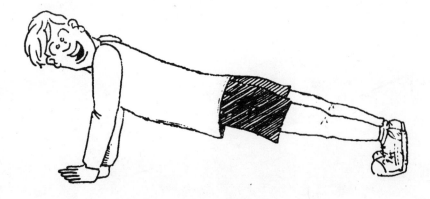

Hello/Good-bye

This exercise is described and illustrated in the parallel sit position, but for variations on a theme, it can be done in the straddle-sit position as well. The child needs to be in a "rocket-ship straight" position with a scooped out tummy as he works his legs and feet. The legs must be perfectly straight at the knees, and this exercise isolates movement at the ankle. He flexes his feet on "hello." This means that he will pull his toes way back towards his body, putting his ankle in flexion. Then he stretches or points them on "good-bye."

After this is executed successfully, the arms can be stretched out parallel to the legs, and hands can do the same as feet. Later for a coordination challenge, the following can be done: hands and feet do opposite, alternate right foot and right hand flex/left foot and left hand point. This makes the exercise akin to the old pat your head and rub your stomach trick. Just make sure that the child is still maintaining a straight back and knees throughout and that his feet are pointing in a nice, straight line. [See illustrations: There must be an equal amount of energy expended by the inner and outer borders of the feet. This produces a correctly aligned foot (Figure C). If the child stretches more on the outside borders of his feet, it will cause his toes to point inward towards each other (Figure B). This is a common mistake because the outer borders of children's feet are naturally loose. If the child stretches more on the inside borders of his feet, it will cause his toes to point outwards, away from each other (Figure A)]. Hello/Good-bye stretches and strengthens the ankles and feet while working on good upper body posture and correct alignment in pointing feet.

Hello, good-bye
Hello, good-bye
Hello, good-bye
Hello, good-bye

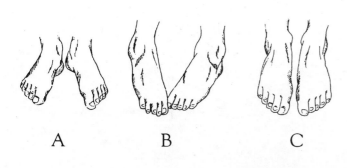

A   B   C

My Sleepy Head

My Sleepy Head is done in the parallel-sit position.   Start sitting up "rocket-ship straight" with "swordfish-straight legs" and "good-bye feet." Nod the head from side to side (ear toward same shoulder), singing, "My head is getting sleepy. It wants to go to bed." Then clap hands and pat tops of thighs on the next line: "I'll clap my hands and pat my legs."

Now start nodding the head again as the torso bends forward and lowers towards legs saying, "And put my head to bed." The child stretches his torso as close as possible to his legs. The lullaby feel of this song reminds you that a stretch should always be a gentle, pulsing movement. One works slowly toward laying the body and head on top of the legs with legs remaining straight and feet pointed.   For variation do the whole stretch with "hello feet." My Sleepy Head is an overall body stretch.

My head is getting sleepy,
It wants to go to bed.
I'll clap my hands and pat my legs,
And put my head to bed.

My head is getting sleepy,
It wants to go to bed.
I'll clap my hands and pat my legs,
And put my head to bed.

Yes, I Do!

Yes, I Do! is an exercise that helps children feel their shoulders pressed down while the rest of their body is pulled up rocket-ship straight. Often when children are instructed to "pull-up" or stand up straight they bring their shoulders up to their ears! This little exercise let's them feel the right way and the wrong way to hold their shoulders. On the words, "I don't know," the shoulders are pulled up to the ears. On "Yes, I do," the child is sitting up perfectly straight with shoulders pulled down, head straight forward and neck long. On "Maybe I do," the child leans his head to the right and pulls up just his right shoulder. On "Maybe I don't," the child leans his head to the left and pulls up just his left shoulder. Finish with a strong, properly pulled-up position on the last, "Yes, I do!" The song is as follows:

> I don't know.
> Yes, I do. (repeat 3 times more)
>
> Maybe I do.
> Maybe I don't. (repeat 2 times more)
> I don't know.
> Yes, I do! (shout this last line and hold the proper position)

I don't know.

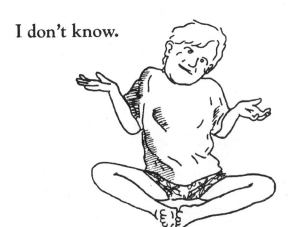

Maybe I don't.

Maybe I do.

Yes, I do!

Basic Locomotor Movement

All dance is built on the eight basic movement steps: the walk, the run, the leap, the jump, the hop, the skip, the slide and the gallop. The accompanying Basic Locomotor Movement chart defines each step fully and precisely, describes how the step is used in daily life (you already know how to do most of them!) and explains how each step is refined to become a dance step.

The first few times you practice each locomotor movement, work only on achieving the correct mechanics of each step. Some children may have difficulty with: making a leap any different from a big running step (It should be suspended in the air longer.), skipping on both feet rather than one (They will do step, step hop instead of step, hop, step, hop. This can be due to a weak ankle or being a strongly one-sided person.), or achieving a true gallop. (A gallop gets both feet up in the air, one right after the other so a short obstacle could be cleared.) Patient coaching and practice will yield results in time. When my younger children four and under joined their older siblings in these sessions, it was not uncommon for it to take a year before the skip, slide and gallop were distinguishable.

As the steps are mastered, then the polish of the dance requirements can be added. The feet should be pointed whenever they leave the ground ("good-bye feet"). The torso must be kept erect ("rocket-ship straight back"), stomach pulled in ("ice cream-scooped tummy") and head, shoulders and hips properly aligned ("roadblock torso"). Varying arm movements and positions can be assigned.

The music provided helps set the tone and establishes the rhythm of each step. For a true aerobic workout, many moms work themselves and their children up to going through all the locomotor movements with the tape, non-stop!

RULE FOR ALL LOCOMOTOR MOVEMENT:

DON'T BUMP INTO ANYBODY OR ANYTHING.

Walk For good imagery, tell the children they are royal kings and queens with crowns upon their heads.

Run Since most children will have already mastered the step, instruct them immediately to run quietly with soft knees, head looking forward and arms still.

Leap Consecutive leaps are difficult to do. Listen to the music and hear: run, run, run, run, run, run, leap.

Jump Always land with soft, bent knees. Then push hard with your feet and legs to get into the air. (Use this same music to hop on each foot. Just a few times! It's hard work.)

March The march is just a stylized walk: knees are brought up high in front, feet are pointed and arms swing in opposition.

Skip Skip alongside a child, holding hands if he has trouble with the rhythm and continuity.

Slide Sliding to the side with the right foot leading, arms stretched out to sides (then reverse to left slides after crossing the room or can be done in a circle).

Gallop It's always the Harris Derby at our house, and my young horses are in the first race of their careers. I play the radio announcer and sometimes hold a broomstick to serve as a jump in the race.

Basic Locomotor Movement Chart

Basic Locomotor Movement		As it would occur in daily life	As it would occur in dance
Terms	Definitions	In daily life, circumstances caused you to move in different ways...	In dance you must learn...
Even rhythm			
walk	transfer of weight from one foot to other, w/ at least one foot always contact w/ floor	When you were about twelve months old, you learned to walk.	correct posture, foot approaches the floor toe-heel instead of heel-toe, arm position will be set
run *to*	transfer of weight from one foot other, w/ a moment when both foot are off floor simultaneously	Hurry!! You're going to miss the bus!!! Run!!!	correct posture, run on balls of the feet, arm position will be set
leap	transfer of weight from one ft. to other occurring in the air; both feet off floor for prolonged time	You are running in the woods, and you come to a small creek. You don't want wet shoes and you're already late for dinner, so you leap across.	hold torso strongly, stretch feet in air, position of legs in air will be set
jump	take off from both feet w/ landing on both feet.	You're at a football game, and your team just scored the winning TD. You throw your popcorn up in the air and start jumping up & down with excitement.	hold torso strongly, stretch feet in air, position of legs will be set
hop	take off from one foot w/ landing on one foot.	Remember playing hopscotch... you can't put your foot down.	hold torso strongly, foot stretches in the air, lifted leg will be set in a position
Uneven rhythm			
skip	a step and a hop, feet change each step	It's your birthday, and you're so excited that you skip happily all the way home...	hold torso strongly, foot stretches in the air, lifted leg will be set in a position
slide	a step and a close w/ transfer of weight in air	Did you ever play any circle games as a child? All hold hands; now everybody slide to the right.	hold torso strongly, reach with the toes on the step, feet stretch in the air and legs come together straight in the air
gallop	a step and a close w/ transfer of weight in air, one foot leads, the other joins	You just saw "National Velvet", "My Friend Flicka" or "Black Beauty" and your friends and you are playing horses. Gallop around the field.	hold torso strongly, reach with the toes on the step, feet stretch in the air

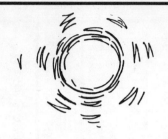

The Four Seasons Interpretation

Here's an example of using movement to reinforce the study of the four seasons. We may use the simple locomotor movement of a walk and place it into typical weather conditions for a season. With the appropriate music playing, narrate with lots of expression the following scenes to your children as they dance and dramatize:

Summer:

"You are walking up a hill on a very, very hot summer day. The sun is beating down on you, and you are dripping with perspiration. Your eyes can barely stay open in the sun's bright glare. Your throat is dry, and you are weary from the heat."

Fall:

"You are walking on a brisk, cool fall day. The wind is blowing against your face in a cheerful, autumny way. The sun is out, and the air is crisp and fresh. You hear the crackle of fallen leaves under your feet as you walk."

Winter:

"You are walking home against the bitter north wind on an icy, snowy cold winter's day. You try to keep your face covered from the chilling winds by huddling down in your winter coat. Still the wind penetrates and keeps you shivering. More snow is falling, and you are walking through slush, snow and ice in different areas. Be careful that you don't slip on a patch of ice!"

Spring:

"April showers . . . you are walking through a field after several days of spring rain. It's pretty muddy, ooey, gooey, slippy, slidey . . . oops! Be careful that you do not fall! Oh, no! Now you are having trouble. Your feet are getting stuck in the mud. Try to get out of it. Just a few more steps. Oh, oh. It's starting to rain again."

Supplemental Exercises

Fun Exercises for Strengthening

Shoulders and Thorax

Creepers / Toddlers / 2s & 3s

The Baby Crawl is done on hands and knees. Baby will learn this one by himself if you leave him on the floor on his tummy and give him plenty of opportunity. It is good for coordination, so even after walking is mastered, use crawling in movement class.

The Russian Bear (See page 8)

The Push-Up Position is a vertical hold on hands and balls of feet. Through observation a small child will imitate this position. Encourage him to do his own brand of push-up (just holding this position is very strengthening).

4s & 5s / 6s & 7s

The Wheelbarrow is a traveling exercise that can take you through the entire house together. The child should get in the Bear-Crawl position and mother grabs his ankles and takes his feet in the air. The child then proceeds to walk on his hands with mom steering him from behind, like a wheelbarrow! Younger children (our twins did this at 22 months), after watching this exercise, want to take the position even though they are not ready to walk it yet. Again, just holding the position is strengthening. Before long they will figure out how to walk on their hands.

The Handstand Roll Out is a step beyond the wheelbarrow. Mother takes feet up so child achieves full handstand position (later let him hold it for awhile) then child bends his arms, tucks his chin into his chest and rolls out (like a somersault). Mother is holding up strongly on child to support his weight (this can diminish as strength is gained) and releases feet only after child's upper back has made contact with the floor.

The Crab Crawl (See page 8)

Blast Off (See page 9)

Push-Ups. Good old-fashioned Push-Ups can be used after the child has gained sufficient strength. They are not as fun as the other shoulder/thorax exercises, but at some point the child may want the challenge of doing a standard exercise. Most children will have to work up to holding a correct position (weight supported on hands and feet, shoulders directly above hands and torso in a straight position). At first they may have to lie on the floor and push up their weight in any way they can. Perfect and polish as time goes on.

Older Children

Handstand Against the Wall. Children of all ages love to be upside down, and an easy way to accommodate that desire is the Handstand Against the Wall. The child can kick up to the handstand, or mother can help him walk over to the against-wall position. Mother can help support the child or merely spot him if he is able to do this himself. Pull him (holding his ankles) upward for a strong, straight handstand position. Work to eliminate the arch in the lower back and protruding abdomen. Stretch the toes to the ceiling (good-by feet!) and stretch the legs (rocket-ship straight!).

The Shoulder Sequence (See page 12)

Handstand Push-Ups can be done in the center of the room or against the wall. The child in a handstand bends his arms and lowers his weight to a headstand position and then pushes back up again. Mother holds his ankles and by pulling up helps him lower carefully to the floor (the descent should be slow and controlled). Then she helps him push back up to the handstand position by pulling up on his ankles.

Legs

Creepers / Toddlers / 2s & 3s

Deep Knee Bends done naturally are for the child preparing to walk. As a child prepares to walk, he may do these using furniture for support or alone. Mother can encourage him to do more and support him (hold his hands and help him up). In the lower position the child will be in a squatting position, and in the higher position he will be standing.

After your child is walking securely, Mother can introduce **Walking Low** (with knees bent) and **Walking High** (on tiptoes). There is no hurry in teaching these; allow the child to become an expert walker first. This is the first locomotor movement that the child learns. (See Basic Locomotor Movement with corresponding chart, pages 17 & 18.) In the Expansion of Locomotor Movement section you will learn how to expand these basic eight into many interesting, fun movement studies.

Point to the Stars is executed while child lies on his back with straight, stretched legs and feet. Make sure body is in correct position with Roadblock (see Fun Exercises for Strengthening the Abdominals pages 26, 27). Child uses his leg as a pointer and raises it up to perpendicular ("Point to the stars.") and lowers it to starting position (alternate legs). This is a slow lift working at keeping form throughout. Use key words: swordfish-straight legs, good-bye feet, roadblock back.

Criss-Cross Apple Sauce is done from the hook lying position on the back (see Standard Positions Chart, page 46.). Bring both knees into chest and then stretch them out to point to the ceiling. The three-word poem is then recited and on "Criss-cross" the legs beat & cross twice. On "apple-sauce" the legs open to a straddle position. Key words for good form: Swordfish-straight legs, good-bye feet, and ice cream-scooped tummies.

Criss   Cross   Apple Sauce

The following are variations on One-Leg Balances designed to strengthen the ankle of the supporting leg while teaching balance:

Marionette Puppet: Mother acts as the puppeteer and gives commands to the child puppet.

For example: "I just pulled the string attached to your left elbow up high; I dropped it. Now I've pulled the string on your right knee. I will leave it up there. I pulled the string on your left hand up high." The idea is to have the child balance on one foot while making his upper body, arms and head do other movement. It's fun and challenging. Be prepared for giggles.

Airplane: The child stands on one leg with the other leg lifted up straight behind him, arms out to the side, & balances. This position is an arabesque in ballet and a form of a scale from gymnastics. Work in degrees to holding the chest up rather than down like a table top, and a swordfish-straight leg in the back with a good-bye foot. To help check on a truly stretched leg, give the command to make the foot a hello foot. This will usually cause the offending bent knee to straighten up.

Bird: Name this balance after your favorite winged friend, perhaps your state bird. It is like an airplane with arms acting as wings flapping gracefully and the supporting leg bends softly and stretches as the bird is in flight. As the child does the balance, mother can go through a guided tour describing the bird's journey: "You have left your nest for your morning flight. It's a lovely sunny day and you ride upon the wind as you fly over fields of wheat. What's that over there? A pretty pool of water, swoop down for a closer look. Now climb back up toward the sky."

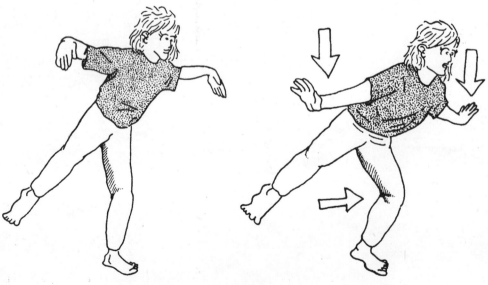

2s & 3s / 4s & 5s / 6s & 7s / Older Children

It is difficult to exercise the legs enough through specific exercises alone. When the child becomes mobile and active, the legs will be well exercised if he plays hard in some of the following ways. If he is not a natural mover, encourage him by supervising and participating. Even a sedentary child can enjoy these activities once he builds up a little strength and stamina.

Using Equipment:

Scooting vehicles: children can use these even before they are walking

Pedaling vehicles: tricycle, big wheels, bicycles

Balance beam: (We never had a real balance beam but my children always made balance beams out of logs, railroad ties, whatever was available.)

        walk forward

        walk backward

        half-turns

        run

        knee bends

Rebounder

Jump rope: Rope turned for the child (If you are short a rope turner, you can tie one end of the rope to something secure and one person can man the rope.)

still snake- People holding the rope make the rope wiggle and slither like a snake. The child is challenged to jump across without allowing the "snake " to touch him.

swing low- People holding the rope let it swing side to side. First the child can leap or jump over it one swing at a time. Later, he can work up to staying in place and jumping over the rhythmic rope every swing.

swing over - People holding the rope swing it in a large circle that will be able to clear the jumper's head at the top and touch the ground at the bottom. The child can first work at running through during the swing. Next step would be to start jumping while the rope is stationary. After that he can run in and start jumping while the rope is moving.

Jump rope: Rope turned by the child

skipping- Child hops one foot and then the other over the rope.

jumping- Child jumps with both feet together over the rope. Be sure to teach him how to add a rhythmic bounce (small jump) in between each big jump over the rope.

crossing- Child can add the crossing of the arms on the downward swing of the rope in front.

double swings- Child quickly swing the rope around twice whilebjumping only once.

Locomotor Movement:

Run

March

Slide

Gallop

Skip

Leap

Jump

Hop

Games:

Hopscotch

Abdominals

Roadblock is an exercise that teaches the body a correct position while lying on the back to help support good posture when standing and moving. It becomes one of our key words to help remind the children of the muscle memory experienced when executing Roadblock successfully. The child starts by lying on his back with knees tucked into chest, then slowly he puts his feet down on the floor to form the hook lying position (See Standard Positions Chart, page 46). While this change of position is taking place, have the child concentrate on:

1. keeping every vertebrae of his spine in contact with the floor,
2. his shoulder blades flat on the floor which opens the chest and sternum for good posture and
3. his tummy pressed down against his back.

If this can be accomplished, he can then be challenged to maintain this position in the torso while stretching out his legs "swordfish straight." Some children will have trouble moving to the hook lying position without arching their backs. Others will not be able to stretch the legs out all the way. Just work to the maximum stretch where good posture is maintained. It's good to hold that position for a long time to train the torso. The child should be breathing normally, concentrating hard but not tense.

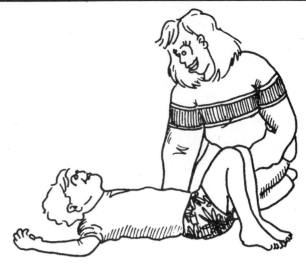

The child tries to maintain thiss correct position, a 'roadblock' as mother attempts to get a 'matchbox car' size vehicle through at the lower back. (Muscle groups work in opposition. When the muscles in the back are stretched out, then the muscles of the stomach will be contracted. This is the desired result here. You can imagine the wrong and opposite look: the stomach muscles are stretched out while the lower back muscles are contracted. Younger children who have little abdominal strength often have that hollowed-out back with protruding stomach that is typically called a sway back.)

Make sure the child's stomach is scooped out flat while contracted. I scoop my hand along the child's stomach as if I were dipping out a scoop of ice cream. Then I use that muscle memory and image of an "ice cream-scooped tummy" to correct a protruding stomach.

Swordfish (See page 10)

Small Hunted Bird is an exercise done lying on the stomach. The child lifts his head, neck and chest off the floor with his arms out-stretched to the sides. He is a bird flying with softly flapping wings. Mother narrates a story about the bird out for his daily flight when a larger predator bird is spotted. This hawk would like to make a late morning snack out of the little bird...so a great chase ensues. The little

child-bird flies quickly now and keeps an eye on the enemy. To do this he twists to the right, centers himself, twists to the left and centers himself again. Then he spots a refuge and swoops into safety. Phew! At this point he lowers his upper body for a needed rest.

Older Children

"Wouldn't That Curl Your Hair?" is a tricky way to slip in good old-fashioned sit-ups with two important improvements. First, the legs are bent in order to minimize strain on the lower back. And secondly, a visual (mother's hand) and a mental (curl your hair) image are provided to help

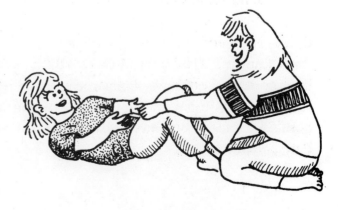

the child execute the sit-up correctly. He will sit up starting with the top of his head and continuing the curl vertebrae by vertebrae from the top down his spine. Child will be lifting just his head, neck and shoulders off the floor. He will lower himself reversing the process, so that the last thing to touch the ground will be his head. So begin with the child in the hook lying position, and mother can sit facing him at his feet. Mother says something like, "If your Daddy came home with his beard shaved off, wouldn't that curl your hair?" On 'curl your hair' she beckons child with her hand and he curls up as described above. Have him hold the position a few seconds; then Mother uncurls her hand saying, "Don't worry, he won't shave his beard," and he can uncurl back down to the starting position. Make up other silly little things and beckon child to the right and left sides of the leg as well as the center in order to strengthen the oblique abdominals.

The V-seat is my best ever, favorite abdominal strengthener. It takes very little space and while building up the stomach, it works the muscles running along the spine as well for good posture. There is no charming poem or song to go with it, just the challenge of doing it and improving it. In the V-sit position, a child works at scooting his heels as close to his seat as possible with the stomach scooped out flat, the back "rocket-ship" straight and his arms wrapped around his legs. Then he releases his legs by stretching his arms out to the side maintaining the straight back and

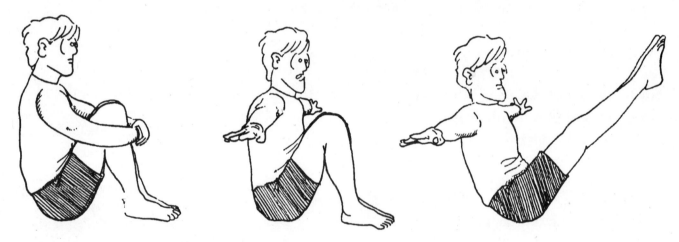

the legs held pressed together. The tendency will be for the legs to open up at the knees and the spine to curve. Mother can press the outside of her calf against the spine to help the child re-establish a straight, tall back. After this is achieved the next step is to stretch the legs out in the air (as in Swordfish), holding one's balance and keeping back as erect as possible. When the stretched out legs are added, the child is working a stretch of the legs at the same time he strengthens the abdominal and erector muscles. Principal dancer with the American Ballet Theatre, Rebecca Wright, who at her prime was considered one of the greatest dancers in the world (this fact was acknowledged by Mikhail Baryshnikov), taught me this exercise when she and I taught at the Dayton Ballet Company's summer school one year. She could do this V-seat, perfectly balanced with her legs pointed straight up to the ceiling and her back held up erect within an inch of her legs. She looked like someone had just folded her in half! That can be the picture that you and the kids work toward.

Fun Exercises for Stretching

Feet and Ankles

Flex & Point Games

Hello/Good-bye: (See page 14)

Warm Your Toes is basically a story to go with the same flex and point exercise in "Hello/Good-bye". In parallel sit position the child reaches his toes (pointed) toward an imaginary bonfire to "warm his toes"; then they get too warm and he draws them back (flexed). Mother narrates the story as it is executed. A sample follows: " It's so cold out tonight. Everybody stretch your legs out closer to the fire. Reach your toes toward the fire. Doesn't that feel great? Now it's getting too hot–pull your toes back." As your family does these and other exercises, you can develop your own stories to go with them. While I work with my children, I make up different ones spontaneously. Sometimes their ideas will help create a new story, song or image for the same old exercise. Let your creative juices flow!

Drawing Circles is an ankle stretching exercise. In the parallel-sit position, the child holds one leg at the knee with both arms and draws the largest circle possible with his toes. Have him do the circle in a clockwise direction and then reverse the circle. Alternate legs. I always encourage my children to see the circle they are drawing: "How big is it? Is it perfectly round?" Make them think of the way a Fourth of July sparkler leaves a momentary drawing of the design it creates. Or let them imagine that their big toe is Harold's purple crayon (a series of children's books that you can borrow from the library if you are not familiar with them) or a piece of chalk.

Walking on Tiptoes is to some children a natural occurrence. Other children can learn if Mom leads the way. I parade around the kitchen and living room on my tiptoes, and my brood easily follows suit. Each child walks up high on the balls of his feet. It can first be done with the knees bending naturally as in a normal walk. And then later the child can walk with stiff, straight knees up on his toes which requires him to pull up tall, strong and upward!

Walking On Heels is a fun, comical thing for children to do that stretches their calves and Achilles' tendon. Child walks on heels, toes in the air. As with walking on toes, this walk can be done with bending knees and then with straight knees.

Legs

In Parallel-Sit Position: The following two are similar stretches that use a song or idea to dress up what would otherwise be a boring old stretch to a child. Since working with my second, third and fourth child, we have already added new ways to do this stretch. Joel came up with a variation on "Tickler"; his idea was the fingers acting like divers preparing to jump off the high dive. The fingers walk down the legs and jump off the "good-bye feet" to land on the floor beyond. The twins like to do "My Sleepy Head" but sing their favorite lullabies instead: we nod for the first part of the song and lay our heads down for the last line. You will be able to develop your own variations as you do these exercises together.

My Sleepy Head (See page 15)

The Tickler is done in the parallel-sit position. Start sitting up "rocket-ship straight" with "swordfish-straight legs" and "hello feet." Hands start on the floor next to hips, and the fingers walk down the outsides of the legs to try to tickle own feet. For variation do the whole stretch with "good-bye feet."

Straddle-Sit Position:

Roll The Ball and stretch your inner thighs and back of the legs at the same time! You and your child sit in a correct straddle position: "rocket ship-straight back", "ice cream-scooped tummy", "swordfish-straight legs," knees on top and "hello feet". That's a tall order right there! Then roll the ball back and forth to one another between the legs and try to maintain a correct position. (More ball handling games in Progression of Eye-Hand Coordination Section)

Erect Starting Position
"Seven-Up"

Seven-up is begun in a correct straddle position: "rocket ship-straight back", "roadblock torso", "swordfish-straight legs" knees on top and "hello feet". The torso will be moving and changing shape, but the legs should remain stationary. Bounce gently to the side six times right ear to right knee counting aloud and them come up and shout "Seven-up!" returning to the starting, erect position.

Ear To Knee

Bounce gently again, this time with the nose to right knee, next time bounce nose to floor in the center between legs, then nose to left knee and lastly left ear to left knee, always bouncing six times and returning to erect position on "Seven-up!" Challenge the children to keep their legs straight, knees facing up to ceiling and feet stretched. Seven-up can be done in frog sit and parallel sit positions as well. (Fitness experts now believe that bouncing is too harsh for the body and the idea of a pulsating, rhythmic movement is better. So I explain it to children as a gentle bounce. Kids understand gentle but would not know what I meant if I told them to pulsate.)

In Other Positions

The Donkey Ride (See page 8)

Nose to Floor
In Center

Hips

These exercises are for turnout (i.e., outward rotation of the legs in the hip socket) and will not be necessary for your children unless you are planning ballet classes in the future or in order to help correct a child who is naturally pigeon-toed. Doing these exercises will help a child maintain the natural flexibility of childhood (if he has it, that is!) or to develop flexibility (if he does not) without having to start out-of-home classes prematurely. The degree that flexibility can be increased diminishes as the child grows older.

Bullfrog on the Back is a holding stretch. Have child start on his back in the hook-lying position with each vertebrae of the spine in contact with the floor (as in Roadblock) and the tummy, ice cream-scooped out flat. Allow the knees to flop open to the sides, soles of the feet together (as in frog sit). Mother can gently press knees open, working up to knees touching the floor. This may seem easy, but the correct position of the torso must be maintained. Watch for an arched back; keep the back flat on floor. By adjusting the closeness of the feet to the hips, the turnout can be worked where the legs are tightest.

Bullfrog on the Stomach is the same holding stretch done on the reverse side. Tell your young dancer that he is a flapjack (pancake), and you are flipping him over. Lying on his stomach, make the child's hips press flat on the floor. Then maintaining the proper torso alignment, the child tries to press his feet to the floor.

Back

These exercises are for stretching the back in different ways: curved, arched and straight.

Monkey On A Broomstick is a gentle, stretching exercise for the back. When the child is strong enough to hang onto a rod or stick, as he holds on lift him off the floor a few inches. The older child can hang on a bar at a playground or a chin-up bar up in a doorway at home to get this stretch.

Small-Hunted Bird: As described in Strengthening Exercises under Abdominals section.

Rocking Horse in the Nursery is done on the stomach. The child takes hold of his ankles with his hands and arches up like a little rocking horse toy. He then rocks himself forward and back.

Blast Off can be done as described in the Musical Accompaniment section, page 9, with the following variations in the beginning and 'blast off' positions: 1) Start in the straddle-sit position to begin. Make sure the back is "rocket-ship straight," the legs are swordfish straight with knees facing up to the ceiling and the feet are in the "good-bye position." Lower the head to the floor between legs for the countdown. Then 'blast off' by rolling back, swinging the legs overhead, trying to touch the ground behind the head with toes. 2) Start in the parallel-sit position to begin with: rocket ship-straight back, swordfish legs and good-bye feet. Lower nose to knees for the countdown. The 'blast off' is a traditional bridge. First the child must in one smooth motion sit up and roll his back gently to the floor so he is lying on his back. Then his arms twist back, and he puts his palms on the ground, his knees bend and he pushes up into a back bend. (See page 37, Tumbling skill section, Bridge) Don't forget that half the fun of all the "Blast off" exercises is counting down out loud and then yelling "Blast Off!!!" at the end. With over twelve years experience of teaching children these exercises, I can state unequivocally that children derive great pleasure from making noise!

Expansion of Locomotor Movement

Once the basic movements are understood and then refined by the standards of dance, many variations and combinations can be done to make them a continual challenge. My examples are merely samples of things that you can do. They do not represent an exhaustive list. Try my suggestions, get comfortable with the different ideas and soon you will be creating your own wonderful movement combinations.

Directional Changes: The locomotor movements can be executed travelling forward, sideways, backwards or turning. These directional changes can be done one at a time and then later combined. Examples: 1) Walk sideways (like a folk dancing grapevine where one foot crosses in front or back of the other) 2) Skip backwards (a difficult move for many children) 3) Skip turning (always a favorite with kids) 4) Walk four steps forward, then pivot, heading in the same direction and walk four steps backwards. 5) Slide sideways with the right foot leading two times, then turning in the air in order to continue in the same direction on the floor, slide sideways with the left foot leading. Switch back and forth like this as many times as space allows. If there are two children who can work together or mom can do with a single child, have them start this exercise facing each other. The children will start with opposite feet leading on the sideways slide. Then when they switch and turn they will be back to back. We sing out "Face-to-face" and "Back-to-back" as we slide. It's fun to turn away from and then turn toward the partner. Once the trick is learned well, the child can hold his one back hand (the same hand as foot that does not lead on the slide) with his partner's back hand. If they both do the turning correctly, they will be able to maintain their hand hold as they go across the lawn or living room!

Stylization: The locomotor movements can be stylized to create a sense of drama or uniqueness. This stylizing also demonstrates to the student that these basic movements really are the foundation of all dance steps. Examples: 1) A favorite stylized walk is a march. It is a walk with an exaggerated bending of the knees lifted high in front, feet pointing down to the ground and arms swinging in opposition. Put on a Sousa march or bark out a military "Hup, two three, four." 2) Stylize a run with feet kicking up in the back or knees coming up in the front. Then try combining the two: four running steps with feet kicked back, then four with knees up in front. Boys can put their hands on their waists (arms akimbo) and girls can swish an imaginary or real skirt.

Level Changes: Level changes are a way to alter the walk and then help the student use math in relationship to his movement which is part of musicality. A basic sequence would be to teach low & high walks separately. Low walks are done with knees bent (as if you were in a room with a low ceiling) and high walks are done on tiptoes (in ballet terms, three-quarter point). Then make combinations of low & high steps: four low and four high. I use my voice to call each step using a change in pitch as well: "Low, low, low, low (bass), high, high, high, high (soprano)." The next step would be one low step and two high steps. And this is a waltz step! Low, high, high. One child can do the steps and another can beat out the rhythm (beat on a drum or clap: strong, soft, soft).

Tempo Changes: Tempo changes are lots of fun and change the size of the movement. Slower tempos equal bigger steps and faster tempos equal smaller steps. A slow laborious walk will be giant steps. A very quick run will be tiny, mincing steps. Alternate slow jumps and quick jumps to illustrate the difference: slow jump, slow jump, quick, quick, quick. A skip done for height will be slow. Have one person skip while the other beats out the tempo of his skip. Then have the drummer or clapper accelerate the tempo and see how the speed diminishes the size of the skip. Make certain that the dancer and the accompanist stay together. This teaches both of them musicality.

Shape Changes: A shape change can be done on many of the locomotor movements to create a different picture in the air. The run can be done with feet kicked up in back. A jump can be done with both legs tucked under (as in frog sit) or with straddled legs (like a cheerleader). A skip can be done with one leg extended straight in back. This is a saute arabesque in ballet.

Create A Floor Pattern: This expansion does not change the step itself but rather directs it in relationship to the pattern it makes on the floor. In a typical home or yard, the child is probably making a straight line pattern from one end to the other. Floor pattern is important to be aware of in order to understand choreography and stage productions. It adds much interest to the simplest movement. Some examples are: galloping in a figure eight (if you have enough children, this can be a challenge learning to cross successfully in the center), sliding sideways in a circle facing the middle of the circle or skipping in a zig-zag. If the child has trouble visualizing the floor pattern, you can mark it out with masking tape or chalk depending on the surface you work on. Verbalize it by having the child imagine that he has stepped into a pan full of fingerpaint and is leaving footprints wherever he travels. You may not wish to use this idea if you have the kind of child who will really want to try it out!

Add Arms and Head: Like the shape changes, adding arms and head will alter the pattern that the child makes while passing through space. A scientific child may appreciate knowing that he is pushing ever so many more molecules of air about with the addition of arm movements. The addition of choreographed arm and head movements requires more coordination and concentration. In a walk or march the child can swing straight arms in opposition to the legs. In other words, when the right leg is forward, then the left arm is forward and vice-versa. This is actually natural but many people will have trouble with it when directed to do so. Be patient. Have the child hold his head looking straight forward, no looking down or to the side. While galloping, the arms can go through three different positions: arms circled at chest height (two gallops), raise to circle framing head (two gallops), opened to sides at shoulder level (two gallops) and remain at sides (two gallops). Repeat. The head can follow the arms with mild tilting: eyes looking into palms of hands when arms are circled in front, eyes & chin lifted slightly upward when head is encircled, head turned alternately right or left as arms open, and head straight forward as arms remain open at sides. This is difficult to coordinate and in ballet is called a port des bras. It is nice to let the children think up their own arm and head movements and challenge the others to dance their creations.

Incorporate An Emotion: This expansion allows children to think about body language. It is amazing to see how much they will know strictly from observation. Tell the child to walk angrily ("Put that ball down and go clean up your room right now!") or walk sneakily (Mom will never know if I just nibble on one of the cookies she just baked.) Or how about run scared, skip joyfully, walk sadly or gallop triumphantly.

Combine Various Locomotor Movement: Another expansion will be combining the various basic steps. Hey! This is really dancing now! One example is to execute three slides forward with the right foot leading and one big skip on the right foot, then continue with three slides forward with the left foot leading and one big skip on the left. The combinations are endless. Students can be given specific steps to include (jumps, gallops and leaps) with the parameter of so many beats. An eight-beat combination could be: gallop sideways three times (a,1,a,2,a,3), jump together (4), jump (5), jump turn (6), leap forward right (7) and then left (8).

Basic Tumbling Skills

This section describes some basic tumbling skills that a child would learn in a pre-gymnastics, tumbling or gymnastics program. These tumbling moves should be done on a mat or carpeted area indoors or on the lawn outdoors. Active children do many of these things on their own. If your children have already attempted these things, here are some guidelines to help gradually improve the moves. Otherwise I do not recommend that you teach them to your children until you have done all the exercises for strengthening and stretching in sequence with obvious results.

Log Roll: The child's body is stretched straight while rolling, arms up above head. The force for the roll comes from the energized stretch of the torso which should be held strongly by the  abdominal muscles. The child should be stiff as a log and try to roll in a straight line.

Tuck Roll: The child's knees are bent to chest with arms hugging them tight. He should keep his knees together and close to his chest throughout the roll.

Forward Roll (Front Somersault): The child begins standing and then squats to floor, placing hands flat on the floor near his feet with knees together bent and tucks his chin into his chest. He then pushes forward and over with legs. The roll should be smooth with a nice curved back. Contact with the floor should take place somewhere between the shoulder blades. Some children may not have a lot of flexibility, and this will make their somersault crash instead of roll. For these kids I would recommend doing them only on very soft surfaces, like a mattress laid on the floor. Make sure the chin is tucked in well to the chest to avoid hurting the neck. I am very cautious with kids doing somersaults. But four of my boys have done them without being taught. So I felt it was important to tell them how to do it safely.

Shoulder Roll: This is a simple roll that almost any child can perform. The child begins in the parallel sit position, then he rocks back and lifts his hips and legs high (with his feet to the ceiling). One knee bends and touches down on the floor near the same shoulder while the other leg remains lifted high. Then he pushes with his hands against the floor near his shoulders and rolls on to the bent knee (the roll is over the shoulder rather than over the back of the head). The ending position is on two hands and one knee with the other leg held up straight in back.

Backward Roll: This is a difficult move which less than fifty percent of the children I have taught in pre-ballet or early gymnastics can execute. I include it because it is basic to gymnastics, but would not recommend teaching it to any child unless he wanted to take gymnastics eventually. It should be done on a mat. The child starts in a standing position and squats, then he sits back and throws his legs over his head and pushes with his hands all in one continuous flow. Important elements to a successful backward roll or somersault are: 1) the hands must twist back, palms flat, fingers pointing toward the shoulders, in order to push the floor, and 2) there must be rolling momentum. As with the forward roll, people with less flexibility in the spine (in this case the flexibility to round over forward) will have trouble achieving this move. Only try it on a soft surface (mattress on floor) and if it is very hard for the child because of a straight back, leave it! If you were considering gymnastics training, this kind of back would indicate that the body was not well suited for the sport.

Cartwheel: The cartwheel is fun motion for children and it seems whenever I see active kids having to wait in a large area like a yard while parents talk or an airport while relatives claim baggage, they are doing cartwheels. To help the child visualize the action in a cartwheel, have him imagine that he is standing in the center of a large wagon wheel (his arms and legs are like the spokes) and the wheel starts to turn. The child begins in a standing position with legs separated and arms stretched out and open above the head. He can rock from one leg to the other to start and then as he rocks onto one leg, he pushes hard with that thigh to throw the weight on the hands which go down one following the other and the feet follow one at a time as the body comes upright.

So a cartwheel to the right would go: right hand, left hand, left foot, right foot. Mother can help by holding a small child at the hips in the upside down position to help him get the feeling and idea of hips over shoulders. These take lots of practice and patience. As confidence and strength develop, the cartwheel will improve. The first ones are real fast with hands going down at once and bent legs barely getting off the floor. In time the legs will stretch out, the hands will touch down one at a time, the line of the body will become more vertical.

Handstand Forward Roll: This difficult move can be done by the not so athletic with the teacher providing support. As described in Strengthening Exercises under the Shoulder/Thorax section, the child kicks up into the handstand position. Mother will catch the child's ankles and help him hold the handstand erect. Then she can allow him to slowly lower his body by bending his arms, tucking his chin into his chest and rolling forward as in a front somersault.

Bridge: The bridge or backbend requires the opposite kind of back flexibility to that required in the forward and backward rolls. In this position, beauty is achieved by an arched back. The child begins by lying on his back. He plants his feet on the floor and places his hands on the floor, palms down and fingers pointing to his shoulders. He then pushes up to a high bridge position. The parent can observe through attempts at the bridge whether the child's back has the ability to arch well. A good bridge will look like a McDonald's golden arch; a poor arch will look like a coffee table. The bridge is not possible by all bodies and should not be attempted without spotting, i.e., support and help by the parent. It requires a flexible back as well as strong arms. Mom can help the child push up and then help support him if needed.

Two ways to come out of the bridge are:
1) Lower gently back down to the ground to starting position.
2) Rock weight forward on the feet and press hips forward, coming up to standing position (keep arms by ears). This is difficult, and mother will need to help press the hips forward and bring up the upper back.

Progression of Eye-Hand Coordination Skills

Indoors or outdoors, playing with a ball is great fun and helps children develop those important eye-hand coordination skills. Use a ball of approximately 6" - 10" inches in diameter. Wonderful balls are available today. We have discovered the Gertie ball which can safely be played with in the house. It is blown up with a straw and is made of a very soft rubber that makes it as gentle as a balloon. It is a great first ball because the children are not afraid of it in play. More durable outdoor balls are available in toy or sports stores and variety stores.

Creepers

Roll the ball Introduce the child to ball play with rolling the ball.
Have your child sit in a correct straddle position (legs rotated outwardly, knees on top and feet stretched) and roll the ball back and forth with him.

Toddlers / 2s & 3s

Toss the ball
    Underhand: Once the child can stand securely, he can learn to catch and throw a simple underhanded toss starting at a short distance with a larger, softer ball.

    Overhand: After the child is successful with the underhand toss, he can be taught to play the same toss game catching and throwing the ball overhand.

Bounce the ball
    Exchange the ball with a bounce in between.

4s & 5s/ 6s & 7s / Older Children

Dribble the ball
    In place: Teach the child to bounce the ball up and down with one hand while remaining stationary. This can be a self-challenging exercise to see how many times one can bounce the ball without losing control of it. As in all these exercises, don't have children compete with each other. They should be working on self-mastery, not comparing themselves to others.
    While Moving: As the child progresses in control and coordination, he can begin travelling with the ball. He is on his way to playing basketball!

Kick the ball

Stationary ball from standing: First the child kicks the stationary ball from a still-standing position.

Stationary ball with run: Next the child runs up to a stationary ball for the kick.

Moving ball from standing: Now mother rolls the ball to the stationary child for the kick.

Moving ball with run: Lastly the child runs up to the moving ball for the kick.

Games

4 square- Use the limitations of boundaries and variations (low ball, high ball, curve balls) to further develop ball-handling skills.

Family-style soccer

Family-style kickball- Rules for this game are just like baseball. The ball is pitched by rolling and kicked with the foot instead of struck with a bat.

Additional ideas:

Other equipment use can be added according to personal resources and preferences: baseball (bat & ball), volleyball (ball & net), tether ball (ball & pole), basketball (ball & hoop), tennis & badminton (ball & racquet), etc.

Academics & Movement

All the exercise and movement studies that you have learned in the previous sections may have already evolved into reinforcement for academic learning. For the younger child, the counting of ball bounces alone can be another math lesson. The ideas that follow are samples of incorporating the movement activity as a reinforcement for other studies. Besides being lots of fun and challenging, these types of activities allow the child to have a sensory memory experience about something important that he must learn. They provide an exercise in which he will be using (in addition to the visual and audio mode) his total body to aid him in remembering a body of information.

In order to help you, I am listing some examples for the younger and older child. Again, these are just samples of things that can be done. You will be able to develop many creative and fun games and new exercises to go along with what you want to teach your children. Use them merely as a springboard for your own imagination.

The Younger Child

Teaching Right and Left

Whenever I have opportunity (putting on clothing, trimming nails, handing child an object), I play right hand or right foot with him. I take his right foot when putting on his socks and shoes and say, "This is your right foot." Then I shake it and wiggle it saying it over and over again. I can also tickle the right foot, put the right foot up high, down low, squeeze it, etc. In a short time a youngster will know his right foot and hand through this game.

Later I will have him do things with his right hand or foot (instead of manipulating it for him): shake it, wiggle it, tickle it, make a fist with it, twist it, put it up high, etc. This game will stimulate his sensory memory, and he will be able to give you his right foot first to step into pants, to put on socks and shoes and his right hand first for putting on shirts. I do not play the game with the left hand or foot. After right is established, I will say, "Give me your right foot." Then "Now, give me your left." (This entire process can be reversed for the left-handed child.)

Teaching Opposites (Antonyms)

I use a little game of freeze poses to teach opposites. A freeze pose is just what it sounds like: a pose is taken, then held. Little ones as well as older children enjoy doing them. I will say, "Show me a pose that is down low." Then, "Take a pose up high." Or, "Make a shape with your body that is open wide." Then, "Now show me a shape that is closed."

Teaching Relationships (Prepositions)

This game can be played two ways: with just the child's body or in relationship to pieces of furniture. It is also fun if you have several children playing it together, and you can get very elaborate. I give commands like: "Put your hands under your feet," or "Place your elbow on top of the piano bench."

This can be done while you are doing dishes, folding laundry or any number of things like that. With several children, you can have them place their body parts in relationship to one another: "Jacob, put your hands on the floor. Sarah, put your back beside Jacob's legs. Rebecca, now you put your feet under Sarah's legs." This can be added to until the children are all wrapped around each other.

Teaching Counting

This is simple to incorporate in any number of ways: I count with my young ones going up and down steps, doing bounces as in the Stretching Exercises under Legs section; use counts for holding a pose (like the one leg balances in the Stretching Exercises under Legs & Ankles section) or strength positions (like the push-up position in the Strengthening Exercises under Shoulder/Thorax section) and counting the number of locomotor steps (example: six skips, then two gallops).

Teaching Seasons and Weather

These games can be used in conjunction with music or literature and are very interpretive. While reading a book on the seasons, we may use the simple locomotor movement of a walk and place it into typical weather conditions for a season.

The Four Seasons (See page 19)

There are so many things to do with the seasons and weather and lots of beautiful music to use. For example: Have the children dance like snowflakes. (You can include discussion about the uniqueness in design of each one and relate that to their own uniqueness.) Make them think of how quietly, how softly, how silently the snow falls. Then allow them to dance like snowflakes to Tchaikovsky's Dance of the Snowflakes from "The Nutcracker."

The Older Child

Teaching Reading

A fun way to review long and short vowel sounds in a phonics study is to use contrasting body shapes. I will talk about the letter 'a' and then its long 'a' sound and its short 'a' sound. On the long 'a' we will stretch out to the parallel sit position with our hands on our ankles (might as well stretch at the same time) and on the short 'a' sound we will pull ourselves in to the V-sit position with our arms wrapped around our knees. Repeat several times and then say words with the short 'a' and long 'a' sounds letting the child take the correct corresponding position: acorn, ant, apple, lake, land, etc. (You can use various contrasting shapes for the other vowel sounds: stretched out long on the floor on one's back vs. knees tucked into chest with arms wrapped around the legs on back or standing on tiptoes, with arms reaching for the ceiling vs. curled up, tiny and small, squatting on the floor.)

Teaching Math

Division: A simple dividing game can be done while bouncing in various seated positions as described in the Stretching Exercises under Leg section: Start with 16 gentle bounces and then change positions (Start with the frog sit, next parallel sit and lastly straddle sit). When you begin again, divide the number of bounces in half. Bounce eight times in each position, then four bounces in each position, then two bounces finishing off with one bounce in each position.

Multiplication Tables: Have the child recite the times table being studied while jumping on the rebounder or jumping rope.

Math Drills: Mom can call out addition, subtraction, multiplication or division problems while the child is in a low-to-the-floor position (like a squat) and when he knows the answer he jumps up and gives it aloud, returning to his original position. This is fun with several students, but I have done it with one child, and it was still an amusing change of pace.

Teaching English

Punctuation: One of the most difficult movement games that Joshua & I used was for reviewing punctuation. We were so tired of the standard drills and practices. So first we 'choreographed' a movement for each punctuation symbol: period = a small jump forward & back with the mouth making a short raspberry sound, comma = body curves in the shape of a comma with the arms overhead, exclamation point = big jump upward with arms shooting straight up, question mark = body does a sideways body wave and sinks to lowered position and with mouth making a 'mmmm' sound, quotation marks = sidebend to left as index and middle fingers 'draw' the marks in the air and with mouth making a 'tsss' sound (at end of quote put the other mark on the right side). Then Joshua would have the chance to study an unpunctuated sentence. Next he would stand up, and as I read the sentence aloud, he would insert the punctuation in the correct places. Shortly, he could do them without reading them before hand. It was fun and challenging!

Parts Of Speech:
Adverbs: Show the student how adverbs modify an action verb. Walk; then walk awkwardly. Run then run leisurely. Skip; then skip gracefully. Jump; then jump frantically. Crawl; then crawl sneakily.

Prepositional Phrases: Show the student how a prepositional phrase will expand or direct a movement: leap in a straight line, hop around the chair, gallop through the hallway.

Teaching Science

I will give you two examples of how I have used movement in science that are very different from one another.

Astronomy (planets and their positions): We used an old sheet to draw our solar system starting with the sun on one side and ending with Pluto on the other side. We used magic markers to do the art work. Then we used the sheet for various movement games: 1) Start on the sun, now jump to the planet that you live on. Next, hop onto your right foot on the planet with the hottest surface. 2) Play a hopscotch game naming the planets as you travel. 3) Play a silly, sure-to-tangle-you-up game. Start on the sun: Put your right hand on earth, place your left hand on Venus. Okay, now put your right foot on Mars. Good, now put your right elbow on Jupiter.

Anatomy (the spine): Describe each type of vertebrae and then make a corresponding body shape: cervical- low & spiny, thoracic - tall & spiny, lumbar - broad, sacrum & coccyx - wide, thick & low. First check student's memory by calling out the vertebrae's name and have him take the appropriate shape & describe it. Then start at the top of the spinal column and walk slowly in the shape of each vertebrae group as you go down the spine: one step for each vertebrae (seven cervical, twelve thoracic, five lumbar and seven sacrum/coccyx). For more challenge try to put in the four natural curves as you walk it out. This is adding a floor pattern!

Creative Expression & Musicality

In the Academics & Movement section you have already seen how a child can utilize movement studies to further explore a subject and interpret through movement ideas like the snow falling and the shapes of our vertebrae. In this section, I will give you examples of movement studies that are related to the arts.

Interpreting Literature

I am giving two examples of movement studies that I have used. The possibilities are endless. As you read your child's favorite books to him daily, think about the energy suggested by the literature. Bible stories provide many opportunities. The lame man who was healed in the name of Jesus Christ by Peter and John went walking and leaping and praising God. In this case the exact steps are given for you. In other stories, the text creates a feeling, and the student can express that feeling through movement. What kind of steps would best represent Daniel as he walked into the lions' den, Joseph as he communicated with his brothers in Egypt, Jacob as he went to meet Esau?

1) The Velveteen Rabbit by Margery Williams, published by Doubleday & Company, Inc., pages 40-41. After reading the book through, reread the last few paragraphs where the rabbit comes to life. Let the child interpret in his movement that great and glorious moment!

2) The Way the Tiger Walked by Doris J. Chacona, published by Simon & Schuster, New York, 1970. Read the following phrases to the child and have him walk like the tiger: "A tiger went for a walk in the jungle . . . (tiger described and pictured). There wasn't a sound, the way the tiger walked." Can he move smoothly, gracefully, quietly, majestically, the way the tiger walked?

Interpreting Music

Introduce him to the classical composers who have created long time favorites for children. Some of these are listed below. Most young children will naturally move to these lovely pieces of music. If the dancing needs more inspiration, offer guidance. ("Make sure you cover all the space in the living room. Be sure to dance high and low. Or include some spins, two freeze poses, skips and leaps.") Also a prop can spice things up. A light chiffon scarf, a skirt for a girl, a cape for a boy, a wand.

Joseph Haydn's fun symphonies "Toy Symphony," "Bear Symphony;"
Robert Schumann's piano pieces for children "Scenes from Childhood," and "Album for

the Young;"

Bela Bartok's children's piano pieces "Sun, Come Out!," "A Hawk Flew on the Branch,"
   "The Grasshopper's Wedding."

Modeste Moussorgsky's "Pictures at an Exhibition," and his children's songs;

Serge Prokofieff's "Peter and the Wolf," and his children's piano compositions, "Music for
   Children;"

Claude Debussey's piano pieces "The Children's Corner;"

Maurice Ravel's "Mother Goose Suite;"

Camille Saint-Saens: "Carnival of Animals"

These pieces will inspire the student to dance. Draw out his movement with questions: "What does that music make you feel like?" "Describe the sounds you hear." "What do you think the composer was thinking about when he wrote this piece?", etc. Help him match the dynamics of his movement and energy to that in the music. This will help him develop artistry as a dancer, musician or patron of the arts.

Interpreting Other Art Forms

1) As we have studied art and architecture in relationship to World History, I have included movement studies. Whether you are studying Gothic cathedrals, medieval castles or Roman columns, individual or group movement studies can reinforce the learning. Use movement to interpret two different styles of Greek art, a vase by Euthymides and one by Euphronios both depicting preparations for battle. The former style is simple and direct; the latter style is graceful and mannered. The student can interpret the story and style simultaneously.

2) Use movement to explore emotions (drama). Take a simple movement like a walk and give it emotion: happy, sad, angry, fearful. Let the child explore what these do to his posture, what kind of energy he uses in association with each one; help him make a clear statement with his body language.

Musicality

All dance will help the child become musical and aware of music. It will tune his ear to listen discriminately to music. I like to use the movement studies to introduce the student to simple music theory. In teaching the locomotor movements of even and uneven rhythms, you will have taught your child how a beat can be divided in different ways to produce different sounds and thereby, different movements. With the use of some visual aids you can help the student understand this more clearly. Examples:

1) Cut out cardboard cards to represent whole notes, half notes, quarter notes and eighth notes. Be sure they are proportionate in size to their value. Use these cards to put together movement studies.

Cards:	□	□	□□	□	❘❘	❘❘	❘❘	□
Counting:	1	2	3 &	4	a 5	a 6	a 7	8
Movement:	walk	walk	run, run	jump together	skip	skip	skip	leap

2) Using geometric symbols make representations of even and uneven steps. Then make measures with these symbols on a card. With these as guides, make a movement study that matches the drawn measures.

Geometric Symbols	○	○	○	△	□	□	□	◇
Steps	slide	slide	slide	skip	walk	walk	walk	freeze pose

Standard Position Charts

hook lying position

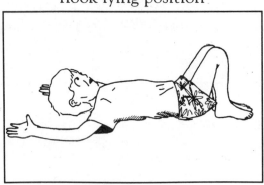

frog sit

parallel sit

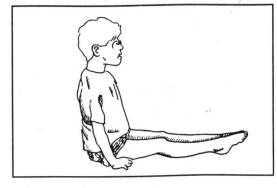

straddle sit

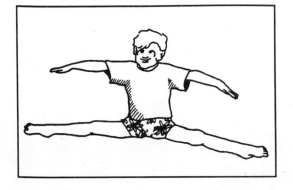

v-sit

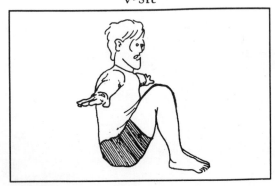

Key Words For Good Form Chart

Form Problem	Key Words for Correcting	Reinforcing Exercise
Shoulders pulled up towards ears, instead of pressed down	"Yes, I do, shoulders"	"Yes, I do!" page 16
Dangling feet with no energy, not pointed	"Good-bye feet"	"Hello, Good-bye" page 14
Bent knees instead of straight legs	"Swordfish-straight legs"	"Swordfish" page 10
Curved, rounded back, not stretched fully	"Rocket ship-straight back"	"Blast-off" page 9
Protruding tummy, abdominal muscles stretched	"Ice cream-scooped tummy"	"Roadblock" page 26
Posture out of alignment (neck, shoulder, stomach hips)	"Roadblock torso"	"Roadblock" page 26